This
**PJ BOOK**
belongs to

PJ Library®

JEWISH BEDTIME STORIES and SONGS

To Max Cohen Osher
and his cousins,
Charlotte Maya Kramer-Cohen
and
Lucas Gordon Kantrowitz
—M.E.

To my dad, mom,
brother, sister,
and Jen
—C.S.

# MAX
# Makes a Cake

by **Michelle Edwards**

illustrated by **Charles Santoso**

Random House 🏠 New York

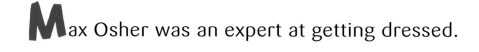

**M**ax Osher was an expert at getting dressed.

He could almost tie his shoes.

And he knew the Four Questions for Passover in Hebrew and English. The other night, he sang them in both languages at the Passover Seder. All by himself. Without any help. The youngest child is supposed to ask them, but Max's sister, Trudy, was a baby. She couldn't even talk yet.

"When you're bigger, you'll have to know the Four Questions for Passover," Max told Trudy. "Why is this night different from all other nights? That's the first one.

"Because on this night, we eat matzoh. That's the answer," said Max. He spooned some smooshed banana right into Trudy's mouth.

"And you'll have to know the Passover story, too.

"A long time ago, the Jews were slaves in Egypt. When Pharaoh freed them, they had to *hurry, hurry, hurry* away with their bread on their backs. The sun baked it flat like crackers. That's what matzoh is.

"Drink up. I have a cake to make."

Trudy tipped over her sippy cup. She spit out her banana smush. Then she pooped.

"Nap time," said Max.

Daddy took Trudy out of her high chair. "I'll be right back," he said.

**"Hurry,"** said Max. "We have a cake to make."

It was Mama's birthday. She was downstairs working in her studio.

While Trudy napped, Max and Daddy were going to make a surprise birthday cake. They'd bought a special Passover cake mix at the supermarket.

"We are going to make a cake," sang Max. "A Passover cake. A birthday cake. A happy-birthday-for-Mama cake."

Max sang his song again. Was Daddy still changing Trudy? Why didn't he *hurry up*?

Max took a sip of milk from
Trudy's cup. All was quiet.

Trudy's door clicked shut.
The upstairs hallway creaked
with Daddy's footsteps.

**"Cake time,"** said Max.

**"Waah! Waah! Waah!"** Trudy cried.

Daddy went back to her room.

Max shook the mix box. Would they still have time to make the cake?

What about the frosting?

They hadn't bought a mix for that. A birthday cake had to have frosting!

Max went to the refrigerator and found some cream cheese and red jam.

He stirred them together. He tasted a fingerful. *Yummy*. It was sweet and pink like frosting. *Very good.* So he made some more.

Now Max and Daddy needed to *hurry, hurry, hurry* to surprise Mama. But Daddy wasn't hurrying at all. What if Mama came upstairs before the cake was done?

"Waah!

Waah!

**Waah!"**

What if Daddy was busy with Trudy all afternoon?

"I don't want to wait anymore," said Max. "I want to make Mama's cake right now."

He smeared his frosting on a piece of
matzoh. Then, before he took even one bite . . .

Max had an idea.

Now all Max needed was a candle. And just as Daddy came in with baby Trudy, he found one.

**"Ta-da!"** said Max.

"Wow, Max," said Daddy. "You did a terrific job!"

"Gurgle, gurgle, goo," said Trudy.

"Let's march to Mama right now," said Max. And he led the cake parade, singing "Happy Birthday" all the way.

Daddy lit the candle. Mama made a wish and blew it out.

Max sang "Happy Birthday" again. Then he sang the Four

Questions in Hebrew and in English.

"Want to know why this cake is different from all other cakes?" asked Max. "Because it's a *hurry, hurry, hurry* Passover cake. And I made it all by myself!"

# How to Make a *Hurry, Hurry, Hurry* Cake

1. Mix some cream cheese and jam together.

2. Taste a fingerful, and add more jam
   if it's not sweet enough.

3. Then spread the frosting on a matzoh.

4. Top with another matzoh.

5. Add more frosting and more matzohs
   until your cake is just right for you.

# The Four Questions for Passover

At the Seder, a special Passover meal, the youngest child asks the Four Questions. The answers help tell the story of Passover.

## The Passover Story

Once, the Jews were slaves in Egypt. Their leader, Moses, said to Pharaoh, "Let my people go." Pharaoh said, "You can go." But then he changed his mind. This happened many times. The last time, the Jewish people hurried out of Egypt. They hurried so fast that the bread they took with them didn't have time to puff up. This flat bread was called matzoh. On Passover, Jews eat matzoh to remember when they were slaves in Egypt, and the thin, hard bread they ate as they journeyed to freedom.

# The Story of Passover—from Your Friends at PJ Library

The first Passover happened long ago in the faraway country of Egypt. A mean and powerful king, called Pharaoh, ruled Egypt. Worried that the Jewish people would one day fight against him, Pharaoh decided that these people must become his slaves. As slaves, the Jewish people worked very hard. Every day, from morning until night, they hammered, dug, and carried heavy bricks. They built palaces and cities and worked without rest. The Jewish people hated being slaves. They cried and asked God for help. God chose a man named Moses to lead the Jewish people. Moses went to Pharaoh and said, "God is not happy with the way you treat the Jewish people. He wants you to let the Jewish people leave Egypt and go into the desert, where they will be free." But Pharaoh stamped his foot and shouted, "No, I will never let the Jewish people go!" Moses warned, "If you do not listen to God, many terrible things, called plagues, will come to your land." But Pharaoh would not listen, and so the plagues arrived. First, the water turned to blood. Next, frogs and, later, wild animals ran in and out of homes. Balls of hail fell from the sky, and bugs, called locusts, ate all of the Egyptians' food.

Each time a new plague began, Pharaoh would cry, "Moses, I'll let the Jewish people go. Just stop this horrible plague!" Yet no sooner would God take away the plague than Pharaoh would shout: "No, I've changed my mind. The Jews must stay!" So God sent more plagues. Finally, when the tenth plague arrived, Pharaoh ordered the Jews to leave Egypt.

Fearful that Pharaoh might again change his mind, the Jewish people packed quickly. They had no time to prepare food and no time to allow their dough to rise into puffy bread. They had only enough time to make a flat, cracker-like bread called matzoh. They hastily tied the matzoh to their backs and ran from their homes.

The people had not traveled far before Pharaoh commanded his army to chase after them and bring them back to Egypt. The Jews dashed forward, but stopped when they reached a large sea. The sea was too big to swim across. Frightened that Pharaoh's men would soon reach them, the people prayed to God, and a miracle occurred. The sea opened up. Two walls of water stood in front of them, and a dry, sandy path stretched between the walls. The Jews ran across. Just as they reached the other side, the walls of water fell and the path disappeared. The sea now separated the Jews from the land of Egypt. They were free!

Each year at Passover, we eat special foods, sing songs, tell stories, and participate in a seder—a special meal designed to help us remember this miraculous journey from slavery to freedom.